BEETLE BAILEY: WORLD'S LAZIEST PRIVATE

Here's another in the happy series of books based on one of the most famous comic strips in the country. Once again the madcap inmates of Camp Swampy valiantly strive to overcome their own ineptitude—and succeed in delighting us on every page.

Mort Walker again gives us a barrel of laughs in his marvelous cartoons concerning the most unprofessional soldier in the army!

Beetle Bailey Books

ABOUT FACE, BEETLE BAILEY
AT EASE, BEETLE BAILEY
BEETLE BAILEY HARD KNOCKS
BEETLE BAILEY ON PARADE
BEETLE BAILEY: OPERATION GOOD TIMES
BEETLE BAILEY: WIPED OUT
BEETLE BAILEY: WORLD'S LAZIEST PRIVATE
BIG HITS FROM BEETLE BAILEY
DID YOU FIX THE BRAKES, BEETLE BAILEY
DON'T MAKE ME LAUGH, BEETLE BAILEY
FALL OUT LAUGHING, BEETLE BAILEY
GIVE US A SMILE, BEETLE BAILEY
I DON'T WANT TO BE OUT HERE
ANY MORE THAN YOU DO, BEETLE BAILEY
I'LL FLIP YOU FOR IT, BEETLE BAILEY
I JUST WANT TO TALK TO YOU, BEETLE BAILEY
IS THAT ALL, BEETLE BAILEY
IS THIS ANOTHER COMPLAINT, BEETLE BAILEY?
I'VE GOT YOU ON MY LIST, BEETLE BAILEY
LET'S CHANGE PLACES, BEETLE BAILEY
LOOKIN' GOOD, BEETLE BAILEY
OTTO
PEACE, BEETLE BAILEY
SHAPE UP OR SHIP OUT, BEETLE BAILEY
TAKE A WALK, BEETLE BAILEY
TAKE TEN, BEETLE BAILEY
WE'RE ALL IN THE SAME BOAT, BEETLE BAILEY
WHAT IS IT NOW, BEETLE BAILEY?
WHAT'S THE JOKE, BEETLE BAILEY?
WHO'S IN CHARGE HERE, BEETLE BAILEY?
WOULD IT HELP TO SAY I'M SORRY, BEETLE BAILEY?
YOU'LL GET A BANG OUT OF THIS, BEETLE BAILEY
YOU'RE OUT OF HUP, BEETLE BAILEY?
YOU'RE ALL WASHED UP, BEETLE BAILEY

WORLD'S LAZIEST PRIVATE

by
MORT WALKER

JOVE BOOKS, NEW YORK

BEETLE BAILEY: WORLD'S LAZIEST PRIVATE

A Jove Book / published by arrangement with
King Features Syndicate, Inc.

PRINTING HISTORY
Jove edition / September 1989

All rights reserved.
Copyright © 1986, 1989 by King Features Syndicate, Inc.
This book may not be reproduced in whole or in part,
by mimeograph or any other means, without permission.
For information address: The Berkley Publishing Group,
200 Madison Avenue, New York, New York 10016.

ISBN: 0-515-10134-6

Jove Books are published by The Berkley Publishing Group,
200 Madison Avenue, New York, New York 10016.
The name "JOVE" and the "J" logo
are trademarks belonging to Jove Publications, Inc.

PRINTED IN THE UNITED STATES OF AMERICA

10 9 8 7 6 5 4 3 2 1